Paddington
in the
Garden

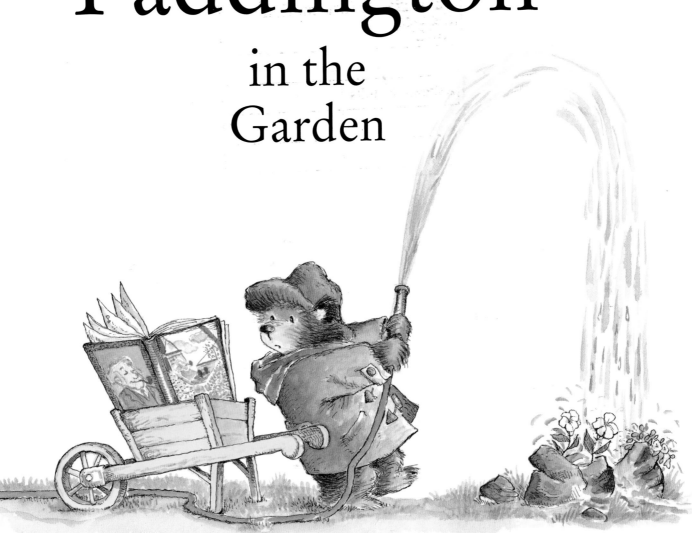

One morning Paddington went out into the garden and began making a list of all the nice things he could think of about being a bear and living with the Browns.

He had a room of his own and a warm bed to sleep in. And he had marmalade for breakfast *every* morning. In Darkest Peru he had only been allowed it on Sundays.

The list was soon so long he had nearly run out of paper before he realised he had left out one of the nicest things of all…

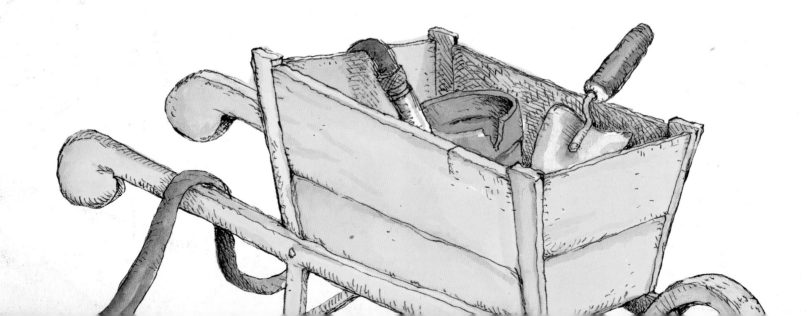

...the garden itself!

Apart from the occasional noise from a nearby building site, it was so quiet and peaceful it didn't seem like being in London at all.

But nice gardens don't just happen. They usually require a lot of hard work, and the one at number thirty-two Windsor Gardens was no exception. Mr Brown had to mow the lawn twice a week, and Mrs Brown was kept busy weeding the flower beds. There was always something to do. Even Mrs Bird lent a hand whenever she had a spare moment.

It was Mrs Bird who first suggested giving Jonathan, Judy and Paddington each a piece of the garden.

"It will keep certain bears out of mischief," she said meaningly. "And it will be fun for Jonathan and Judy as well."

Mr Brown agreed it was a very good idea, and he marked out three plots at the far end of the lawn.

Paddington was most excited. "I don't suppose there are many bears who have their own garden!" he exclaimed.

Early the next morning all three set to work.

Judy decided to make a flower bed and Jonathan
had his eye on some old paving stones.

Paddington didn't know what
to do. In the past he had often
found that gardening was much
harder than it looked, especially
when you only had paws.

In the end, armed with a jar of Mrs Bird's home-made
marmalade, he borrowed Mr Brown's wheelbarrow
and set off to look for ideas.

His first stop was a stall in the market, where he bought a book called *How to Plan Your Garden* by Lionel Trug.

It came complete with a large packet of assorted seeds, and if the picture on the front cover was anything to go by, it was no wonder Mr Trug looked happy for he seemed to do most of his planning while lying in a hammock. By the end of the book, without lifting a finger, he was surrounded by blooms.

Paddington decided it was very good value indeed – especially when the owner of the stall gave him two pence change.

Mr Trug's book was full of useful
hints and tips.

The first one suggested that before
starting work it was a good idea to close
your eyes and try to picture what the garden
would look like when it was finished.

Having walked into a lamppost by
mistake, Paddington decided to read
another page or two, and there he found
a much better idea. Mr Trug advised
standing back and looking at the site
from a safe distance, preferably
somewhere high up.

He knew just the spot.

By the time Paddington reached the
building site near the Browns' house
it was the middle of the morning, and
the men were all at their tea break.

Placing his jar of marmalade on a wooden
platform for safekeeping, he sat on a pile of
bricks for a rest while he considered the matter.

There was no one about…

And there was a ladder nearby…

Mr Trug was quite right. The Browns'
garden did look very different from high up.
But before he had time to get his breath back,
Paddington heard the sound of an engine
starting up. He peered through a gap in the
boards. As he did so his eyes nearly popped out.

On the ground just below him, a man was
emptying a load of concrete on the very spot
where he had left his jar of marmalade!

Paddington scrambled back down the ladder as fast
as his legs would carry him, reaching the bottom just
as the foreman came around a corner.

"Is anything wrong?" asked the man. "You look upset."

"My jar's been buried!" exclaimed Paddington hotly,
pointing to the pile of concrete. "It had some of Mrs Bird's
best golden chunks in it, too!"

"I won't ask how your jar got there," said the foreman, turning to Paddington as his men set to work clearing the concrete into small piles, "*or* what you were doing up the ladder."

"I'm glad of that," said Paddington, politely raising his hat.

Suddenly there was a whirring sound from somewhere overhead, and to Paddington's surprise the platform landed at his feet. "My marmalade!" he exclaimed thankfully.

"Your *marmalade*?" repeated
the foreman, staring at the jar.
"Did you say marmalade?"
"That's right," said Paddington.
"I put it there ready for
my elevenses. It must have
been taken up by mistake.
Now the top's come off!"

It was the foreman's turn to look as though he could hardly believe his eyes.

"That's special quick-drying cement!" he wailed.

"It's probably rock-hard already – ruined by a bear's marmalade! No one will give me tuppence for it now!"

"I will," said Paddington eagerly. "I've had an idea!"

Paddington was busy for the rest of the week.

When the builders saw the rock garden he had made, they were most impressed, and the foreman even gave him some plants to finish it off until his seeds started to grow.

"It's National Garden Day on Saturday," he said. "There are some very famous people judging it. I'll spread the word around. You never know your luck."

The foreman was as good as his word,
and on Saturday half the neighbourhood
turned up at number thirty-two Windsor
Gardens to see the judges arrive.

Paddington nearly fell over backwards
with surprise when he discovered that
no less a person than Mr Lionel Trug
himself was leading the procession.

"It's very good of you to get out of
your hammock, Mr Trug!" he exclaimed.
    "Er…not at all," said Lionel Trug.
"My pleasure. I must say, I love your
orange stones. Where *did* you find them?"
    "I didn't," said Paddington.
"I think they found me.
Thanks to the builders."

"Congratulations!" said Mr Trug, as he handed Paddington a gold star. "It's good to see a young bear taking up gardening. I hope you will be the first of many."

"Who would have believed it?" said Mr Brown, as the last of the crowd departed.

"You must write and tell Aunt Lucy all about it," said Mrs Bird. "They'll be very excited in the Home for Retired Bears when they hear the news."

Paddington thought that was a good idea, but he had something to do first.

He wanted to add one more important item to his list
of all the nice things there were about being a bear
and living with the Browns:

HAVING MY OWN ROCK GARDEN!

Then he signed his name and
added his special paw print…
…just to show it was genuine.

Paddington

at the
Carnival

One day, Paddington's friend Mr Gruber took him
on a surprise outing to a part of London known
as 'Little Venice'.

"It's called Little Venice because it's by a canal,"
he explained, "and every spring they hold a big Carnival.
Boats come from all over the country to take part
in the celebration."

Paddington always enjoyed his days out with Mr Gruber.
He waved as one of the boats went past. All the people
on board waved back.

"I've never been for a ride on a canal before," said Paddington.

"Who knows," said Mr Gruber mysteriously, "perhaps you will before the day is out. But first of all, we must see what else is happening. We don't want to miss anything important."

He pointed to a board showing all the different events,
but there were so many, Paddington didn't know which
to try first.

"How about the Busy Bee Adventure Trail?" suggested
Mr Gruber. "You have to find as many things as possible
beginning with the letter B."

Paddington thought that sounded like a very good idea,
especially when Mr Gruber told him the first prize was
a free boat ride for two.

"Bears are good at trails, Mr Gruber," he explained.

Looking around he could already see lots of things
beginning with the letter B. Apart from B for BOARD,
there was a BOY blowing BUBBLES, a man eating a
BAGEL, and another with a BROOM, a BARBECUE,
and a lady selling BANANAS. There were BOATS
everywhere and lots of BALLOONS. There was even
a man playing the BANJO in a BAND.

After Paddington had finished writing them all down, he and Mr Gruber set off along the canal.

In no time at all, Paddington had added five other items to his list: first there was B for BRIDGE, and then BLACKBIRD, BUTTERCUP, BLOSSOM and BUTTERFLY.

They hadn't gone very far when they saw a lady feeding
some ducks.

   She was wearing a BONNET, a BLOUSE fastened
at the neck with a BROOCH and around her wrist
she wore a BRACELET.

When she saw Paddington she smiled and said, "Would you like some?"

"Thank you very much," said Paddington. He wrote down BAG and BREAD. He then raised his hat politely and said, "Busy Bee Adventure Trails make you hungry."

"This is the sort of day out I like, Mr Gruber!" Paddington announced, as he took a jar of marmalade from his suitcase and began making a sandwich.

"Ahem, Mr Brown." Mr Gruber gave a cough. "I think you were really meant to give the bread to the ducks."

Before Paddington had time to reply, there was a loud buzzing noise and something landed on his marmalade.

Paddington gave the object a hard stare before adding BEE to his list.

Next, they came upon a nice man fishing.

"I think you've struck lucky, Mr Brown," whispered Mr Gruber.

He waited patiently while Paddington wrote down BOX, followed by BERET, BEARD, BELT, BUCKLE, BOOTS, BUCKET and BASKET.

"Would you like to have a try?" asked the man. You can use some of my worms if you like."

Paddington thought that was a very good idea, but first he wrote B for BAIT.

"If you're going in for the Busy Bee competition," said the
man, "you should watch out. There's a boy following you
and I think he's up to no good."

Paddington was about to say "thank you" when he felt
a tug on the fishing line. "I think it might be too big to
go in my jar, whatever it is!" he exclaimed. "It feels like
W for WHALE."

"I'm not sure you'll find any whales this far inland, Mr Brown," said Mr Gruber tactfully.

All the same, to be on the safe side, Mr Gruber tied some rope around his friend.

"Strike me pink!" said the fisherman. "It's a BICYCLE!"

Paddington was most disappointed.

"Never mind," said Mr Gruber. "At least it's another word for your list."

Shortly afterwards, they came
upon a stretch of water with high
banks and trees on either side.
Paddington decided to have a go
at riding the bicycle. But he soon
discovered why it had been
thrown away.

"I think I'd better hold the
other end, Mr Gruber," he
gasped, pointing to the rope still
tied around his waist. "In case
I fall in the canal."

Mr Gruber was about to
explain that if he did that,
there would be nothing for
anyone else to hold on to, when he saw
the look on Paddington's face.

"Is anything the matter, Mr Brown?" he asked.

"I think we're being followed by a B for BUSH,
Mr Gruber," hissed Paddington.

"Come back!" shouted Mr Gruber. "Whoever
you are!"

Meanwhile, Paddington added BINOCULARS
to his list.

While he was writing, a boat went past and one of the passengers had a BABY on her lap. She was feeding him from a BOTTLE. The baby was wearing a BIB and his sister was holding a BALL.

Mr Gruber sat down by the water while Paddington added up his list.

Altogether, with the BANK and BRAMBLES next to Mr Gruber, he had forty-one things beginning with the letter B.

Mr Gruber looked at his watch.
"I think it's time we got back,
Mr Brown," he said. "We don't
want to be late for the judging."
"Good luck," called the
fisherman as they went past.

"We shall be
cheering you on,"
said the lady feeding
the ducks.

"Has anyone collected more than forty B's?" called
the judge.

"I have!" cried Paddington, waving his piece of paper
excitedly. "I've got forty-one."

"So have I!" came a voice from nearby.

Mr Gruber looked over the boy's shoulder. "This list
is exactly the same as young Mr Brown's," he said sternly.
"You must have been copying it word for word!"

"Oh dear," said the judge. "We can't have that.
I'm afraid I shall have to stop the contest!"
"It's all right, Mr Gruber!" called Paddington.
"We've won. I've thought of another B.
That gives me forty-two."

"Fancy nearly forgetting the most important item of all,"
said Mr Gruber, as they set off on their boat trip.
"What made you think of it?"

"I saw my reflection in the water," explained Paddington.

Mr Gruber nodded. "It's often the hardest of all to see things
that are right under your nose," he said.

"It is if you're a B for BEAR," agreed Paddington.
"Bears have very long noses."

It was dark by the time Paddington and Mr Gruber arrived back, and the fireworks had already started.

Mr Gruber bought a packet of sparklers and, as they stood on the bridge to watch, Paddington joined in with his own display.

With his sparkler, he waved

Thank you, Mr Gruber for a lovely day out.

In the excitement, the only person who noticed was Mr Gruber himself, but that was really all that mattered.

"If you ask me, Mr Brown," said Mr Gruber, as they made their way home, "the nicest B of all is yet to come."

"I think I know what that is," said Paddington sleepily. "It's B for BED!".

Paddington
and the Grand Tour

One morning Paddington answered the door bell at
number thirty-two Windsor Gardens and to his surprise
he found his best friend, Mr Gruber, waiting outside.

"I've decided to treat myself to an outing, Mr Brown,"
he said, "and I was wondering if you would care to
join me?"

Paddington was very excited. He always enjoyed
his days out with Mr Gruber and he didn't need
asking twice.

In no time at all he returned with his
suitcase full of marmalade sandwiches
ready for the journey, along with Mrs
Bird's umbrella in case it rained.

They hadn't gone very far when Paddington spotted a bench. "Perhaps we ought to eat our sandwiches now, Mr Gruber," he said. "If it rains they might get wet."

While they had stopped Mr Gruber showed Paddington some photographs of the places he wanted to visit.

"I thought we might go on what's called a Hop On – Hop Off bus," said Mr Gruber.

"You can come and go as you like, so it's possible to see lots of different sights with only one ticket."

"I don't think I've ever been on one of those before," said Paddington as they went on their way. "It sounds very good value."

But as they turned a corner and Paddington saw the waiting bus he nearly fell over backwards with alarm, for part of the roof was missing.

"I think the driver must have gone under a low bridge by mistake!" he exclaimed.

Mr Gruber laughed. "Don't worry, Mr Brown. It's made that way so that the passengers have a good view of the sights. If you wait here and form a queue," he continued, "I'll get the tickets. Then we can make sure of seats in the front row."

"That's a good idea," said an inspector. "The early bird catches the worm and I'm expecting a large party of assorted overseas visitors any moment now."

"Perhaps I can interest you in one of these booklets telling you all about the trip," said the inspector. "It comes in lots of different languages."

Paddington was most impressed. "Thank you very much," he said. "I'd like one in Peruvian, please."

"Peruvian!" repeated the man. "I'm afraid we don't get much call for that."

"You don't get much call for it?" exclaimed Paddington. "Everybody speaks it in Darkest Peru. You don't even have to call out."

He gave the man a hard stare.

"Wait here," said the inspector nervously. "I'll see what I can do."

No sooner had the inspector disappeared than Paddington saw a
crowd approaching, so he raised Mrs Bird's umbrella in case he
had a job finding him again.

"I'm sorry we're late," panted the leader of the group.
"We got held up."

Paddington politely raised his hat. "That's all right," he began. "We can't all be early birds. I'm forming a que…"

Before he had time to say any more he found himself being pushed to one side as there was a mad scramble to board the bus.

Paddington watched in dismay as everyone on the top deck began fighting for the front seats.

"I wouldn't sit there if I were you," he called. "There may still be some worms." But he was wasting his breath, so he tried again. "Excuse me," he called. Lifting one leg, he waved the umbrella. "It's a Hop On bus and I'm afraid the two front seats upstairs are reserved."

"Hold it, you guys!" The leader gave a loud blast on his whistle. "You're supposed to hop everywhere, OK? Pass it down the line."

"What happens now?" came a voice, when everyone was settled.

Paddington considered the matter for a moment. "I'm not sure," he replied. "I shall need to ask Mr Gruber, but I think you look at the view, then you hop off again."

"View?" wailed someone. "What view?"

Their voices were lost in the general commotion as the leader blew several more blasts on his whistle and issued fresh instructions.

"I came on this trip to see the sights," protested a lady as she staggered off the bus, "not become one!"

"I'm worn out," gasped another, collapsing into her husband's arms, "and we haven't been anywhere yet!"

A number of passers-by stopped to watch and several children joined in the fun.

Soon the whole pavement was alive with figures.
Paddington tried closing his eyes, but whenever
he opened them more people had arrived.

He was very relieved when he spied a familiar figure pushing his way through the crowd towards him.

"Are you all right, Mr Brown?" called Mr Gruber. "This place looks like a battlefield."

"It feels like one, Mr Gruber," said Paddington. "I was trying to save our seats in the front row, but I'm afraid I wasn't quick enough."

"The inspector gave me this booklet," said Mr Gruber. "He said he's very sorry it's in English, but he suggested we find somewhere quiet to read it until the fuss had died down. There's a little café over there. I'll hurry on ahead and reserve a table."

Mr Gruber hadn't gone very far before Paddington felt a spot of rain on the end of his nose, so he stopped to open the umbrella. Almost immediately he heard a whistle and a voice shouting, "Follow him, you guys! Don't let him out of your sight!"

Paddington hurried on his way as fast as his legs would carry him. Even so, he only just managed to reach the café ahead of the others.

"Quick, Mr Brown," hissed a voice from behind some potted plants. "Over here. There's some cocoa on its way."

"I should be careful with your sips, Mr Brown," warned
Mr Gruber as the waitress arrived with two steaming mugs.
"It looks very hot and they may give the game away."

"I don't know about my sips, Mr Gruber," gasped Paddington, as the crowd burst through the door. "I'm beginning to wish I'd brought my disguise outfit."

"There you are!" cried the leader. "I've never known a tour captain so hard to keep up with."

"Tour captain?" repeated Paddington.

"You were holding up your umbrella…" said the man. "That's what tour captains always do. It's so that people don't get lost."

"I'm not a tour captain," said Paddington, hotly. "I'm a bear."

The crowd fell silent as they took in the news.

"You mean we've been doing all that hopping around for nothing," complained one of the party. "I thought it was some quaint old English custom."

"What are we going to do now?" cried someone else. "We've missed our bus!"

Paddington looked out of the window at the rain and then at his booklet. "I think I've got an idea coming on," he announced.

After explaining what he had in mind, he waited for the others to settle down. Then, while Mr Gruber held up his pictures one by one, Paddington read from the booklet.

If the words didn't always match up with the pictures no one seemed to mind, and at the end, as the sun came out again, they all applauded.

"That was the best tour I've never been on," said someone amid general agreement.

"I didn't know Buckingham Palace was over 60 metres high," said a lady as the party began to leave.

"I'm afraid it got mixed up with Nelson's Column by mistake," explained Paddington. "It's a bit difficult with paws and I must have turned over two pages at once."

"Never mind," said a man. "The exercise has done us all good. I haven't felt so fit in years."

And to show how pleased they were, everyone dropped a coin or two into Paddington's umbrella as they went past.

"Well," said Mr Gruber, when it was all quiet again. "What do you think of that, Mr Brown?"

"I think," said Paddington, "I might become a tour captain when I'm old enough. It seems a very good job for a rainy day. Especially if you have your own umbrella!"